ULTIMATE STICKER COLLECTION

LEGO minifigures

W9-CCV-344

HOW TO USE THIS BOOK

Read the captions, then find the sticker that best fits in the space. (Hint: check the sticker labels for clues!)

•

Don't forget that your stickers can be stuck down and peeled off again.

•

There are lots of fantastic extra stickers too!

LONDON, NEW YORK,
MELBOURNE, MUNICH, AND DELHI

Written and edited by Shari Last and Lisa Stock
Designed by Rhys Thomas

First published in the United States in 2012 by
DK Publishing
375 Hudson Street,
New York, New York 10014

10 9 8 7 6 5 4 3 2 1

001–183880–Jun/12

ISBN: 978-0-7566-9251-3

Color reproduction by MDP, UK
Printed and bound by L-Rex Printing Co., Ltd, China

Discover more at
www.dk.com
www.LEGO.com

Series 1

MINIFIGURES LIKE TO have fun. And when you mix a Cheerleader, a Ninja, a Magician, and all their crazy friends, there's a whole lot of fun to be had! Watch out for the Circus Clown though, not everyone agrees with his idea of fun!

GREETINGS EARTHLINGS! I COME IN LEGO PIECES.

Deep Sea Diver
The Deep Sea Diver explores the depths of the ocean, discovering amazing creatures.

Magician
Prepare to be amazed as the Magician shows off his most incredible trick—disappearing into thin air!

Nurse
When minifigures get sick the Nurse always knows how to make them feel better.

©2012 LEGO

Zombie

Not quite alive and not quite dead, the Zombie slowly lumbers around, frightening everyone he meets.

©2012 LEGO

Ninja

A Ninja is supposed to be a stealthy warrior. But not this minifigure —he is a bit too clumsy!

©2012 LEGO

Caveman

Other minifigures have nice LEGO houses. But this prehistoric man prefers his LEGO cave.

©2012 LEGO

Super Wrestler

The Wrestler's mask hides his identity because his loyal fans would recognize him anywhere.

©2012 LEGO

Forestman

This medieval hero loves to defend castles and rescue princesses with his trusty bow and arrow.

©2012 LEGO

Tribal Hunter

The Tribal Hunter uses his tracking skills to find missing objects.

Spaceman

The Spaceman never takes off his spacesuit and helmet… even when he is on Earth!

©2012 LEGO

©2012 LEGO

Skater

The Skater loves to try out dangerous stunts. He only worries about injuries to his cool board!

©2012 LEGO

Robot

The Robot is programmed to build, build, build! He never gets tired.

©2012 LEGO

Cheerleader

No team can lose when the Cheerleader cheers it on with her pom poms.

©2012 LEGO

Circus Clown

The Clown has a joke for every occasion. Be careful though— he thinks it's funny to squirt people with water.

©2012 LEGO

Series 2

WHO SAYS DIFFERENT minifigures can't be friends? The Pharaoh, the Vampire, the Karate Master, and their various friends don't have much in common, but they always find something fun to talk about. Even the Mime tries to join in!

SURF'S UP! WHAT DO YOU SAY?

Skier

The skier often ends up with a face full of snow, but it doesn't get him down. He gets right back up and tries again.

...

Karate Master

This martial arts expert wears his black belt with pride. He can smash bricks with his bare hands! Ha-ya!

©2012 LEGO

6

Traffic Cop

The Traffic Cop makes sure that all the LEGO vehicles obey the rules of the road.

Pharaoh

The Pharaoh rules Ancient Egypt. He feels lost without any pyramids around. Maybe the Robot could build one for him?

Spartan Warrior

This Ancient Greek soldier always wears his helmet so he is ready for battle.

Disco Dude

The Disco Dude is addicted to music! He would dance all day and all night if he could.

Weightlifter

The Weightlifter wants to prove he's the strongest man in the world. He can lift anything —or anyone!

Pop Star

This super star regularly tops the music charts and jet sets around the world singing to all her fans.

©2012 LEGO

Maraca Man

Shake, shake, shake! The Maraca Man gets people tapping their feet to his rhythmic beat.

Lifeguard

The Lifeguard sits in her beach tower, keeping an eye on the minifigures swimming in the ocean.

©2012 LEGO

Mime

This silent performer uses his hands and facial expressions to tell you exactly what he's thinking.

©2012 LEGO

Explorer

The Explorer travels to exotic places hoping to discover sights, animals, and plants to tell his friends about.

©2012 LEGO

Ringmaster

Roll up! The dapper Ringmaster is the leader of the circus and he encourages the crowd to cheer and shout.

©2012 LEGO

Witch

The Witch has magic powers, but she only uses them to help people. Mostly...

©2012 LEGO

Series 3

MINIFIGURES LIKE TO keep fit, and sport is a great way to stay healthy and have some fun— just ask the Snowboarder. Even the less sporty minifigures find ways to keep fit, like fishing, racing through space, or dancing the Hula.

©2012 LEGO

Baseball Player
For this sportsman, baseball is everything! His favorite moment is when he hits a home run.

Fisherman
The Fisherman has been on many high seas adventures. He has lots of crazy stories to tell.

©2012 LEGO

Tribal Chief
The Tribal Chief is a respected leader and warrior. He takes his tribe on many exciting adventures.

©2012 LEGO

Elf
Can you spot the Elf camouflaged among the brown trees of the forest? He's guarding his village against intruders.

©2012 LEGO

Samurai Warrior

This brave soldier is a master of ancient Japanese sword fighting. He uses his skills to help people in need.

©2012 LEGO

Hula Dancer

The Hula Dancer teaches other minifigures how to perform the traditional Hawaiian dance moves.

Mummy

Minifigures beware! The Mummy is known for casting annoying curses.

Gorilla Suit Guy

Look closely at this minifigure. This is no gorilla—it's a guy in a gorilla suit!

WOW. ALIENS CAN RAP!

Snowboarder

The Snowboarder travels the world, searching for the coldest, steepest mountain to snowboard down!

Sumo Wrestler

The Japanese Sumo Wrestler is very strong. He takes on lots of huge opponents in the Sumo ring.

Pilot

The Pilot is happiest when he is flying his plane thousands of feet in the air. He never wants to come back down to Earth.

AHH... MR MONKEY, MY OLD NEMESIS, WE MEET AGAIN.

Race Car Driver

The Race Car Driver has a need for speed! He'll drive any vehicle—as long as it goes fast.

Rapper

The Rapper creates music all the time, turning words into a rhyme.

Space Villain

This evil mastermind is feared across the galaxy. Look out—he might be plotting to conquer your planet.

Space Alien

After his busy outer space travels, this alien enjoys his stay on Earth—it is such a fun planet!

Tennis Player

The Tennis Player uses her talent and her lucky racket to win every tennis match she plays.

Series 4

LOTS OF THESE minifigures have special talents. The Artist paints amazing pictures and the Street Skater performs incredible skateboard tricks. The Lawn Gnome is an expert at keeping still for a long time. What is your talent?

ARE YOU READY TO ROCK?

Street Skater
The cool Street Skater thinks walking is boring! He skates across the city, showing off with his amazing skills.

Hockey Player
The Hockey Player is an ice hockey champion. However, he needs to learn that winning isn't everything!

The Monster
There's no need to be scared of this Monster—he is helpful and friendly.

Crazy Scientist

The Crazy Scientist's lotions and potions bubble away as he carries out his mad experiments. They don't always go according to plan…

Kimono Girl

The Kimono Girl wears her traditional Japanese robe with pride. Her folding fan keeps her cool in summer.

Soccer Player

The Soccer Player enjoys being part of a team, but he likes winning trophies, too.

Lawn Gnome

This minifigure is not a regular Lawn Gnome. He sometimes gets bored of standing still and wanders off!

I'D LIKE TO PAINT YOU!

Ice Skater

The Ice Skater dances across the ice elegantly and gracefully to music.

Sailor

Land ahoy! The Sailor loves life at sea. He can spot land from miles away thanks to his trusty telescope.

Hazmat Guy

If you spill a dangerous substance, call the Hazmat Guy! He will put on his airtight protective suit and make everyone safe.

Surfer Girl

Sun, sand, and surfing —what more could you want? The Surfer Girl never tires of riding the waves.

Artist

The Artist paints his beautiful pictures on any surface he can find, from rocks to walls.

Punk Rocker

It's always noisy when the Punk Rocker's around. He loves playing his electric guitar really loudly!

Musketeer

The Musketeer is one of the best swordsmen in France. He likes nothing better than to test his skills in a duel. On guard!

Viking

This strong, fearless warrior is ready to defend his tribe from invading trolls, dragons, and sea monsters.

Werewolf

When the full moon rises, the Werewolf becomes half-man, half-wolf. He tries to be scary, but no one ever runs away!

COME BACK! LET'S SEE WHAT THIS POTION WILL DO!

AARGHH!

Series 5

SOME MINIFIGURES, LIKE the Detective, are good at solving problems. But others are more likely to create problems! The Lizard Man and Evil Dwarf get up to lots of mischief, much to everyone's amusement.

I SUPPOSE IT'S FISH AGAIN FOR DINNER TONIGHT!

Graduate
It's graduation day and the Graduate is proud to hold his college diploma. Now he has to get a LEGO job!

Small Clown
Watch out for the Clown's favorite joke —a pie in the face!

Lizard Man
Underneath his costume, the Lizard Man is just a regular minifigure… who dreams of being a giant monster.

Cave Woman

The Cave Woman is so busy making tools and catching food, she doesn't even have time to wash her face!

Boxer

The Boxer is famous for his fast fists. He is a LEGO champion!

Lumberjack

Timber! The Lumberjack spends all day chopping trees to build log cabins.

Zookeeper

The Zookeeper loves all animals—even the crazy dragons in Cage 101 at LEGO City Zoo!

Royal Guard

The Royal Guard protects the palace. He takes his job very seriously and never smiles—even when the other minifigures try to make him laugh!

Gangster

Don't be deceived by his smart suit. The Gangster is still a sneaky criminal who rules the underworld of LEGO City.

Detective

To solve a great mystery, call the Detective. He uses his magnifying glass to follow the clues.

Egyptian Queen

All hail the beautiful Queen of Egypt! She wants to build the tallest LEGO pyramid in the world!

Snowboarder Guy

The Snowboarder knows lots of facts about snow! Well, he does spend a lot of time on it!

Ice Fisherman

The Ice Fisherman drills holes in the ice to catch fish.

Fitness Instructor
Time to exercise! The Fitness Instructor is determined to keep everyone around her fit and healthy.

Gladiator
The Gladiator bravely battles warriors and beasts in a giant, circular arena.

Evil Dwarf
This bearded bully will battle for any cause... if you offer him the right price.

FOR MY NEXT VICTIM...

DON'T EVEN THINK ABOUT IT!

Series 6

MINIFIGURES ALWAYS HAVE plenty to do. Some work hard to become Mechanics or Surgeons, while others ask a Genie to make their dreams come true. Not everyone wants to keep busy, though… the Sleepyhead is happy to stay in bed!

Genie
Rub the magic lamp and the Genie will appear to grant your wishes. Choose them wisely —you only get three.

Bandit
The outlaw robs and cheats his way around the Old West. But the sheriff is bound to catch him sooner or later.

Classic Alien
The Alien is stranded on Earth. Can you build him a spaceship to take him back to his home planet?

Highland Battler
This minifigure defends his Scottish homeland. He scares enemies away with his angry expression.

Flamenco Dancer

The Flamenco Dancer loves the sound of traditional Spanish music. She dances and claps her hands to the beat.

Intergalactic Girl

Space is not a scary place when the Intergalactic Girl's around. She keeps the cosmos safe with her quasar zapper.

TICK TOCK

Leprechaun

This little Irish Leprechaun has hidden his pot of gold. Quickly find out where it is before he disappears!

SO, WHAT SEEMS TO BE THE PROBLEM?

Butcher

The Butcher thinks about meat all day long! He even dreams about steaks and burgers!

Roman Soldier

March on! This Roman is the best soldier in his legion. He practices his battle skills day and night.

Minotaur

This half-minifigure, half-beast is rarely seen. He lives deep inside a labyrinth and often can't find his way out!

I'LL JUST HIDE MY POT OF GOLD... UH OH...

Clockwork Robot

Wind him up and watch the Clockwork Robot work. But as he starts to unwind he gets slower and slower…

Skater Girl

The Skater Girl's tricks and stunts are so cool, the Skater and the Street Skater are among her many fans.

Mechanic

The Mechanic can fix any LEGO vehicle. No job is too big or too small!

Sleepyhead

Is it morning already? The Sleepyhead wishes he could snooze in bed all day with his teddy bear.

Surgeon

The Surgeon carries out tricky operations on her patients with great skill.

Lady Liberty

Lady Liberty is a symbol of hope. She inspires all of the minifigures to do their very best.

Series 7

THE MINIFIGURES ENJOY many different hobbies, from swimming and singing, to visiting their LEGO relatives. Some take their hobbies very seriously, like the Tennis Ace, but luckily the Hippie is at hand to help everyone relax.

Bagpiper
The Bagpiper enjoys learning to play traditional Scottish music, but he can also play disco tunes!

Aztec Warrior
Don't mess with this ancient Mexican warrior. He is serious about protecting his treasure.

Jungle Boy
The Jungle Boy enjoys his simple life, swinging from vines with his monkey friends.

Viking Woman
While her husband is out battling monsters, the Viking Woman also works hard. She hunts for food and builds the family's longboat.

Bride
The Bride is dressed in a beautiful white gown. She is so excited for her special day!

Daredevil

The Daredevil has no fear! He'll jump through flaming hoops and leap across deep ravines —just for fun!

Evil Knight

The Evil Knight roams the LEGO kingdom, looking to cause mischief. Minifigures beware!

Tennis Ace

The Tennis Ace is very competitive. When he is playing a match, he doesn't take notice of anything else!

WHO ARE YOU CALLING GRANDMA?

OH GRANDMA, WHAT BIG EARS YOU HAVE!

Hippie

The Hippie likes to take it easy. He wants his minifigure friends to relax too, so he often brings them flowers and tea.

Computer Programmer

Has your computer crashed? Call the Computer Programmer. He'll know how to fix the problem.

Rocker Girl

The Rocker Girl loves to play loud guitar music more than anything else. Rock on!

I HAVE TRAVELED ALL THE WAY FROM THE OTHER SIDE OF THE GALAXY.

FAR OUT!

Galaxy Patrol

Members of the Galaxy Patrol protect outer space from dangerous aliens, invaders, and space villains.

Swimming Champion

The Swimming Champion loves making a splash! She's good at winning swimming races, too.

Bunny Suit Guy

Bunny Suit Guy loves wearing his fluffy bunny suit with its big, floppy ears. He eats carrots and hops about all day.

Ocean King

The Ocean King rules the seven seas. He uses his golden trident to create storms, huge waves, and whirlpools.

Grandma Visitor

This little girl brings her grandma cakes and cookies every week. She also brings a treat for her grandma's pet wolf.

Your LEGO World

THE LEGO WORLD is a place of excitement and fun! Minifigures love getting together with their friends to discuss their hobbies and adventures. Who are your favorite minifigures? Find them and create your own amazing LEGO scene.

IT'S A GOOD DAY FOR A BATTLE.

OR A PARTY!

Build Your Own

WHAT CRAZY combinations can you create? Mix and match the stickers of different minifigure parts. Choose from your favorite characters and see what amazing minifigures you can dream up!

HOW ABOUT A ROMAN ROBOT FLAMENCO DANCER?

©2012 LEGO

?

?

?

?

?

?

?

Zombie

Hula Dancer

Lawn
Gnome

©2012 LEGO

©2012 LEGO

Viking

©2012 LEGO

©2012 LEGO

Tennis
Player

©2012 LEGO

©2012 LEGO

Boxer

©2012 LEGO

©2012 LEGO

Cheerleader

©2012 LEGO

Mechanic

Bandit

©2012 LEGO

©2012 LEGO

G.T

©2012 LEGO

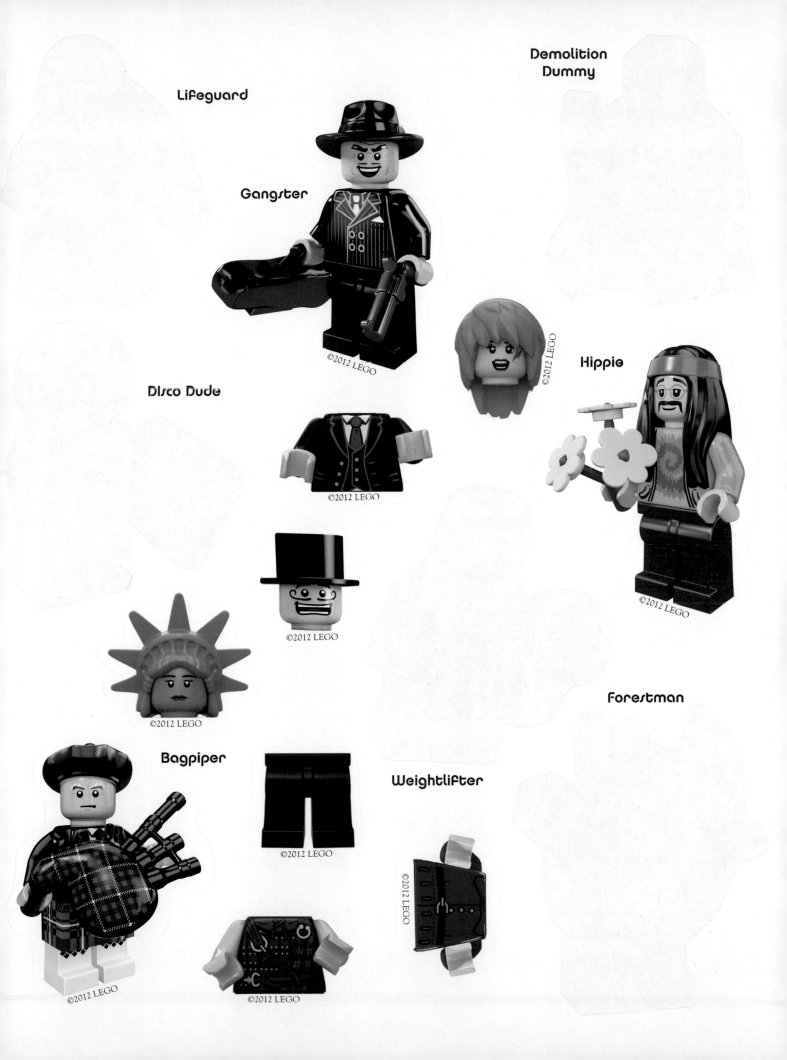

Lifeguard

Demolition Dummy

Gangster

Disco Dude

Hippie

Forestman

Bagpiper

Weightlifter

©2012 LEGO

Skier

Evil Knight

©2012 LEGO

©2012 LEGO

©2012 LEGO

©2012 LEGO

©2012 LEGO

©2012 LEGO

Skater
Girl

©2012 LEGO

©2012 LEGO

Fitness
Instructor

©2012 LEGO

©2012 LEGO

©2012 LEGO

Lizard
Man

©2012 LEGO

©2012 LEGO

The
Monster

Surfer Girl

©2012 LEGO

©2012 LEGO

Tribal Chief

©2012 LEGO

©2012 LEGO

Pop Star

Tennis
Ace

©2012 LEGO

©2012 LEGO

©2012 LEGO

©2012 LEGO

©2012 LEGO

Highland
Battler

Swimming Champion

Evil Dwarf

©2012 LEGO

©2012 LEGO

©2012 LEGO

©2012 LEGO

Space
Villian

Lady Liberty

Bunny Suit Guy

Daredevil

©2012 LEGO

©2012 LEGO

©2012 LEGO

Pharaoh

Sleepyhead

©2012 LEGO

Gladiator

©2012 LEGO

©2012 LEGO

©2012 LEGO

©2012 LEGO

©2012 LEGO

Cave Woman

Leprechaun

Ice Skater

©2012 LEGO

©2012 LEGO

©2012 LEGO

©2012 LEGO

©2012 LEGO

Gorilla
Suit Guy

Surfer

Cowboy

Vampire

Super
Wrestler

Rapper

Circus
Clown

Mime

Traffic
Cop

Flamenco Dancer

Deep Sea Diver

©2012 LEGO

©2012 LEGO

©2012 LEGO

Aztec
Warrior

©2012 LEGO

Karate
Master

©2012 LEGO

Grandma
Visitor

Nurse

©2012 LEGO

Spaceman

Ice
Fisherman

©2012 LEGO

©2012 LEGO

©2012 LEGO

©2012 LEGO

Clockwork Robot

Explorer

Kimono
Girl

©2012 LEGO

©2012 LEGO

©2012 LEGO

Punk
Rocker

Baseball
Player

©2012 LEGO

©2012 LEGO

Intergalactic
Girl

©2012 LEGO

Race Car
Driver

Skater

Musketeer

©2012 LEGO

©2012 LEGO

©2012 LEGO

©2012 LEGO

Maraca
Man

Pilot

Elf

Magician

Hockey
Player

Bride

©2012 LEGO

©2012 LEGO

©2012 LEGO

©2012 LEGO

©2012 LEGO

©2012 LEGO

©2012 LEGO

Lumberjack

Butcher

Surgeon

©2012 LEGO

©2012 LEGO

©2012 LEGO

©2012 LEGO

©2012 LEGO

Artist

Egyptian Queen

Tribal Hunter

©2012 LEGO

©2012 LEGO

©2012 LEGO

Jungle Boy

Ringmaster

Spartan Warrior

©2012 LEGO

©2012 LEGO

©2012 LEGO

©2012 LEGO

©2012 LEGO

©2012 LEGO

Genie

©2012 LEGO

Viking Woman

©2012 LEGO

Minotaur

©2012 LEGO

©2012 LEGO

Computer Programmer

Sumo Wrestler

Samurai Warrior

Fisherman

Snowboarder

Space Alien

Ocean King

Sailor

Hazmat Guy

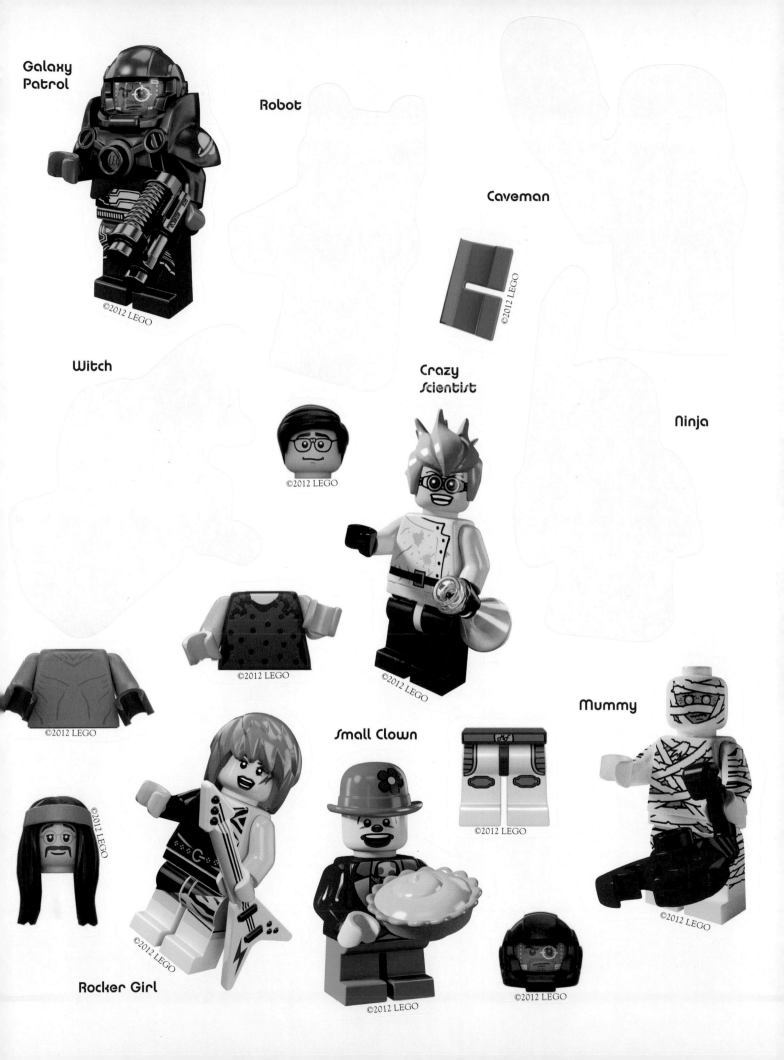

Galaxy
Patrol

Robot

Caveman

Witch

Crazy
Scientist

Ninja

Mummy

Small Clown

Rocker Girl

©2012 LEGO

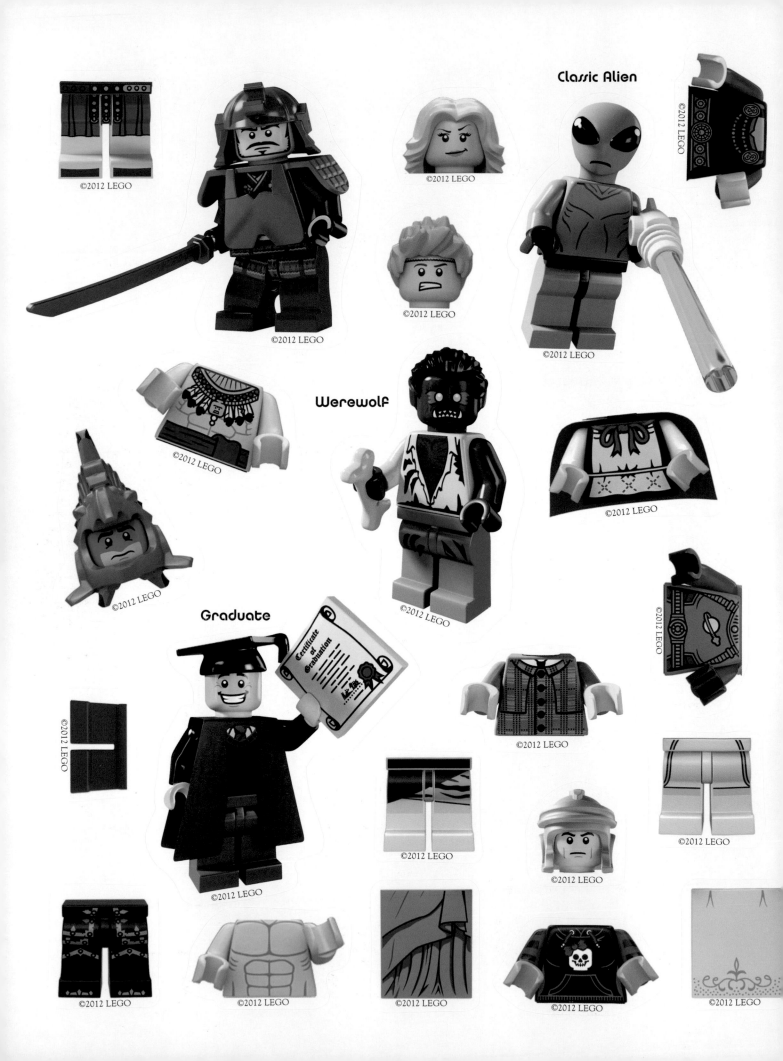

Classic Alien

Werewolf

Graduate

©2012 LEGO

Street
Skater

Detective

©2012 LEGO

Soccer
Player

©2012 LFGO

Roman
Soldier

©2012 LFGO

Snowboarder
Guy

©2012 LEGO

Royal
Guard

©2012 LEGO

©2012 LEGO

©2012 LEGO

©2012 LEGO

©2012 LEGO

Zookeeper

©2012 LEGO

©2012 LEGO

©2012 LEGO

Extra Stickers

©2012 LEGO

©2012 LEGO

©2012 LEGO

©2012 LEGO

©2012 LEGO

©2012 LEGO

©2012 LEGO

©2012 LEGO

©2012 LEGO

©2012 LEGO

©2012 LEGO

©2012 LEGO

©2012 LEGO

©2012 LEGO

©2012 LEGO

©2012 LEGO

Extra Stickers

©2012 LEGO

©2012 LEGO

©2012 LEGO

©2012 LEGO

©2012 LEGO

©2012 LEGO

©2012 LEGO

©2012 LEGO

©2012 LEGO

©2012 LEGO

©2012 LEGO

©2012 LEGO

©2012 LEGO

©2012 LEGO

PA7 70

Extra Stickers

©2012 LEGO

Extra Stickers

©2012 LEGO

©2012 LEGO

©2012 LEGO

©2012 LEGO

©2012 LEGO

©2012 LEGO

©2012 LEGO

©2012 LEGO

©2012 LEGO

©2012 LEGO

©2012 LEGO

©2012 LEGO

Extra Stickers

©2012 LEGO
©2012 LEGO
©2012 LEGO
©2012 LEGO
©2012 LEGO
©2012 LEGO
©2012 LEGO
©2012 LEGO
©2012 LEGO
©2012 LEGO
©2012 LEGO
©2012 LEGO
©2012 LEGO
©2012 LEGO

Extra Stickers

©2012 LEGO

©2012 LEGO

©2012 LEGO

©2012 LEGO

©2012 LEGO

©2012 LEGO

©2012 LEGO

©2012 LEGO

©2012 LEGO

©2012 LEGO

©2012 LEGO

©2012 LEGO

Extra Stickers

©2012 LEGO
©2012 LEGO
©2012 LEGO
©2012 LEGO
©2012 LEGO
©2012 LEGO
©2012 LEGO
©2012 LEGO
©2012 LEGO
©2012 LEGO
©2012 LEGO
©2012 LEGO
©2012 LEGO
©2012 LEGO

Extra Stickers

©2012 LEGO

Extra Stickers

©2012 LEGO

©2012 LEGO

©2012 LEGO

©2012 LEGO

©2012 LEGO

©2012 LEGO

©2012 LEGO

©2012 LEGO

©2012 LEGO

©2012 LEGO

©2012 LEGO

©2012 LEGO

©2012 LEGO

©2012 LEGO

©2012 LEGO

©2012 LEGO

©2012 LEGO

Extra Stickers

©2012 LEGO

Extra Stickers

©2012 LEGO
©2012 LEGO
©2012 LEGO
©2012 LEGO
©2012 LEGO
©2012 LEGO
©2012 LEGO
©2012 LEGO
©2012 LEGO
©2012 LEGO
©2012 LEGO
©2012 LEGO
©2012 LEGO

Extra Stickers

Extra Stickers

©2012 LEGO

Extra Stickers

©2012 LEGO

Extra Stickers